For John and Gay,
a couple who wear their long hair and
flares on the inside.

CONOR McHALE lives in Dublin. Out of every week he spends forty-nine hours sleeping, forty hours working as an archaeologist, thirty-one hours with his wife Susannah and their son Oscar, twenty-one hours writing and illustrating, seven hours cooking, six hours visiting friends and extended family, five hours in the bathroom and three hours dithering. This adds up to a grand total of one hundred and sixty-two hours. There are one hundred and sixty-eight hours in a week. If you find Conor's missing six hours either store them in a time-saving device or spend them wisely.

This is Conor's third book in the FLYERS series. He has also written and illustrated *Jigsaw Stew* and *Don't Open that Box!*

O'BRIEN flyers

FLYER books are for confident readers who can take on the challenge of a longer story.

Can YOU spot the aeroplane hidden in the story?

Fishbum and Splat

Written and illustrated by
Conor McHale

THE O'BRIEN PRESS
DUBLIN

First published 2001 by The O'Brien Press Ltd,
12 Terenure Road East, Rathgar, Dublin 6, Ireland.
Tel: +353 1 4923333; Fax: +353 1 4922777
E-mail: books@obrien.ie
Website: www.obrien.ie
Reprinted 2003, 2007.

ISBN: 978-0-86278-735-6

British Library Cataloguing-in-Publication Data
McHale, Conor
Fishbum and Splat. - (O'Brien flyers ; 10)
1.Children's stories
I.Title
823.9'14[J]

3 4 5 6 7 8 9 10
07 08 09 10

The O'Brien Press
receives assistance from

Typesetting, layout, editing, design: The O'Brien Press Ltd
Printing: Cox & Wyman Ltd

CHAPTER 1

The Hook

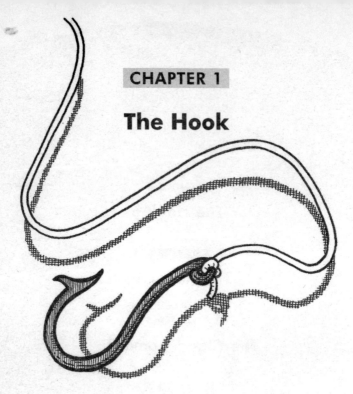

The stars in Heaven were twinkling.

Far below in Hell the eyes of two demons twinkled back.

'I love stars,' said the demon called Fishbum.

'I wish we had some down here,' said the one called Splat.

They were sitting in their favourite
spot, on top of a broken television set.
It had fallen through the roof of Hell
when they were small. The hole it had
made was perfect for star-gazing.

Older demons said it had
come from Heaven.
Something to do with
dancing angels!

'Stars in Hell?' said Fishbum. 'No, thank you! Stars **explode** if demons touch them.'

Just then, something hard and shiny walloped off Splat's head.

'What was that?' asked Fishbum.

'That was **sore**,' said Splat.

They scrambled after whatever it was.

It bounced into a corner and lay there, shimmering.

'It's ... it's an ice cube!' gasped Splat. 'And it's **mine**!'

'No, it's mine,' said Fishbum, trying to grab it. 'You can get your own – when Hell freezes over!'

'Why is there a fish-hook stuck in it?' said Splat.

'Oh no!' said Fishbum. 'Drop it. It's **demon-bait**!'

But they couldn't drop it. They were already caught.

ZOOM! The ice cube shot into
the air with the two demons
frozen on to it.

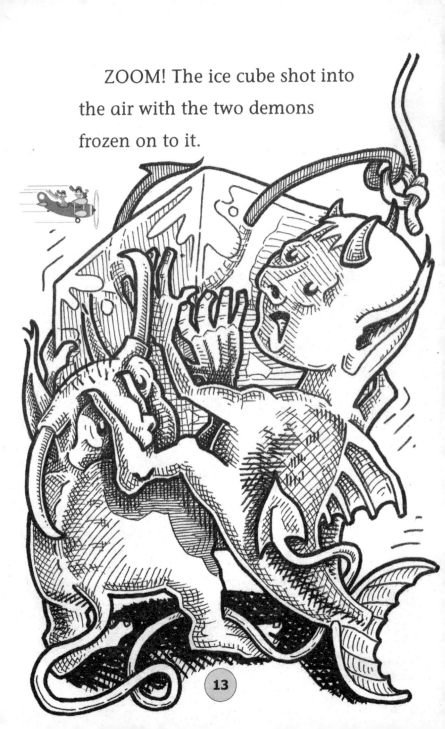

'What's demon-bait?' squeaked
Splat.

'Angels fish for demons with it!'
answered Fishbum.

'You mean we've been caught
by an **angel**?'

Fishbum tried to answer –
but his mouth was full
of cloud.

CHAPTER 2

The Angel

By the time Fishbum had coughed up
all the cloud and said: 'Yes, an angel,'
they were already looking at one.

'Wow! **An angel**!' repeated
Fishbum.

'He's huge, and look at that
necklace,' shivered Splat.

'Stars!' gasped Fishbum. 'If we
touch one of those – boom!
It's curtains for us.'

The angel danced from foot to foot.
'Two demons! I caught two demons,'
he bellowed, while his dog barked
with excitement.

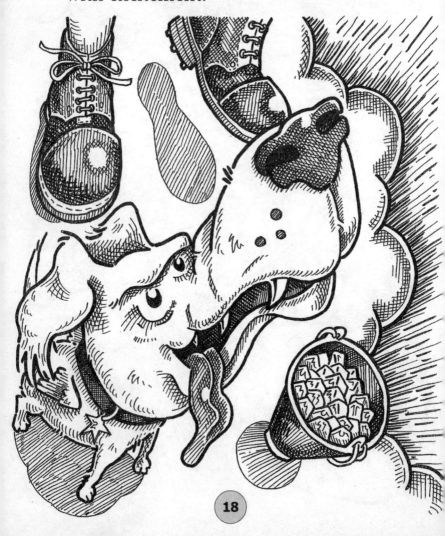

'Look, he's dancing,' said
Splat, staring at the angel's huge
boots. 'Remember our television
in Hell? Didn't dancing angels
put it there, or something like
that?'

Fishbum didn't answer.
He was looking at **the dog**.

The dog looked hungry. And with
a demons-for-dinner shine in his eyes,
he leapt and made a snap at them.

'Down, boy!' shouted the angel, but it was too late. The dancing angel tripped and his necklace broke. He fell with a crash in a **shower of stars**.

The angel stood up and gathered all his stars into his pocket.

Then he looked for the demons
– under his robe, under his
hobnail boots, even under
his dog.

He couldn't find them.
They had disappeared.

With a sulky look on his face, the angel gave up searching and headed for home.

On the way, the demons noticed that he couldn't stop dancing. He just loved it. Jigs here, reels there, the odd pirouette. If this angel was anything to go by, Heaven was full of dancing.

CHAPTER 3

The Cloud–home

The angel arrived home and leapt gracefully into an armchair.

'Any luck?' asked his mother, dancing up to him.

'I caught two, but they escaped,' he grumbled.

One of the stars in the angel's pocket fell out and rolled behind a cushion. But Fishbum and Splat didn't notice it – they were gaping at the star necklaces all the angels were wearing. The thought of touching one made them **sweat**.

What they **did** notice was that
the angels danced all the time.
Standing up or sitting down, they
waved their arms and stomped
their feet.

'Now that we're all here, turn up that radio,' yelled the father angel. 'Turn it up good and loud.'

The radio was turned up and weird, screechy music came out.

'It sounds like a bag of cats,'
said Fishbum.

'Sounds like there's a hedgehog
in the bag too,' added Splat.

It sounded awful, but the angels seemed to like it. Within moments they were all on their feet dancing like maniacs.

The parents waltzed, the grandfather did a two-step, the children whirled and twirled. Not a soul was left sitting.

For Fishbum and Splat it was a
nightmare. Their angel was dancing
so fast they began to lose their grip
on his wings.

'I can't hold on!' whimpered
Fishbum.

'If you let go now you won't be dogfood or popcorn. You'll be a **pancake**!' shouted Splat.

But Fishbum had already let
go and fallen into the throng of
boots below.

'**Fishbum**!' cried Splat –
and he let go too.

CHAPTER 4

The Angel-boot Rodeo

The floor was like a forest of stamping boots.

'Watch out!' shouted Splat, pulling Fishbum sideways as a boot banged down.

'This is disastrous,' wailed Fishbum. 'Things couldn't be worse!'

Then more stars began to spill out of their angel's pocket on to the floor.

'It's just got worse!' howled Fishbum. 'Watch out!'

'We must get up on one of the boots! It's our only chance,' cried Splat.

Boom! Another boot came down and a star bounced by.

'Quick !' cried Splat, dodging a
star. He leapt on to the boot with
Fishbum behind him.

Whoosh! the boot took off.

Bang! Whoosh! Bang! Whoosh!
went the boot as it swung to the
music.

'I'm slipping,' cried Splat.

'Hold on!' said Fishbum. 'I
have an idea.' He pulled at the
angel's bootlace.

The lace undid and the boot flew off the angel's foot. It soared across the cloud and landed on the armchair.

'Hooray, we're safe!' shouted Fishbum.

But he was **wrong**. They were in more danger now than they ever had been.

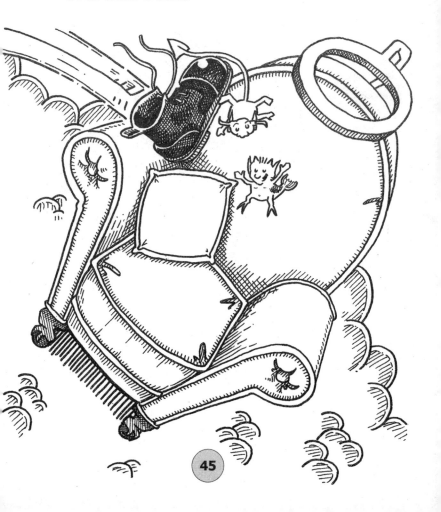

The angels' dancing was becoming
so wild that they needed more space.

'Get that furniture out of the way!'
roared the mother.

The angels pushed all the
furniture to the edge of their
cloud-home. Fishbum and Splat's
armchair ended up right at the
very edge of the cloud.

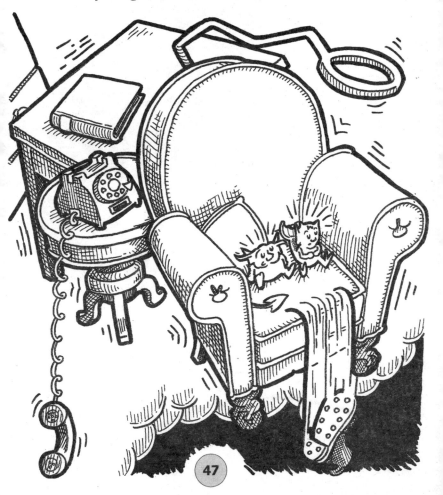

The dancing started up again and the whole cloud began to shake. The armchair jolted and rattled until it was teetering at the cloud's edge ...

'Uh oh!' said Splat. 'Now I know how that television ended up in Hell.'

The cloud shook once more. The armchair slipped and hurtled Hellwards ...

CHAPTER 5

Straight to Hell

'We're in deep trouble,' said Fishbum. 'Do you think we should **pray**?'

Mountains and treetops rushed by.

'You've spent too long in Heaven,' said Splat. 'Demons don't pray, remember? Anyway, I think I can do something here.'

'What?' said Fishbum.

Bushes and grass whizzed past.

'Why are you called Fishbum?'
asked Splat.

'Haven't a clue,' said Fishbum.

'Ever wonder why **I'm** called
Splat?' said Splat.

'Why?' said Fishbum. Hell was only seconds away.

'It's all to do with that television ...' said Splat.

He scuttled underneath the armchair. The roof of Hell burst open as they plummeted through.

Fishbum closed his eyes. He expected an almighty bang, but instead there was a sudden stop, with a squishy 'splatting' noise.

He climbed down. Splat had broken the fall.

'I'm called Splat,' he wheezed,
'because when I was little that
television landed on me. And if I
survived **that**, why not **this**?'

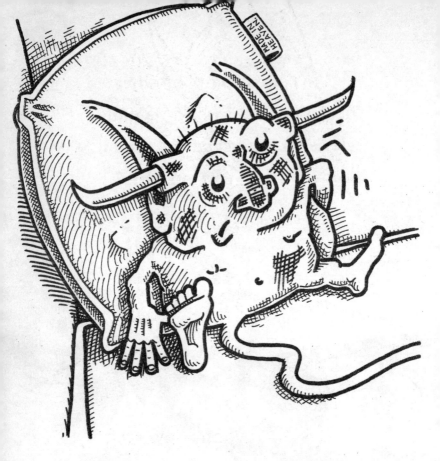

Fishbum helped Splat climb
back on to the armchair.

'So **that** was Heaven,' said
Splat, with a puzzled look on
his face.

'Give me Hell any day,' said
Fishbum.

'Why is this armchair so
uncomfortable?' said Splat,
reaching under the cushion to see
what was making it lumpy.

Fishbum leapt into the air.
'Drop it! Run!' he shouted. 'It's
going to **explode**!'

Splat was too petrified to move.

'We'll blow up like fire-
crackers,' roared Fishbum. 'Boom!
Goodbye! End of story!'

But Splat still didn't move. He was scared stiff.

'Can't you hear me, Splat?' shouted Fishbum. '**Explode**! Explode! Ex ... Why isn't it exploding?' He stopped ranting and touched the star.

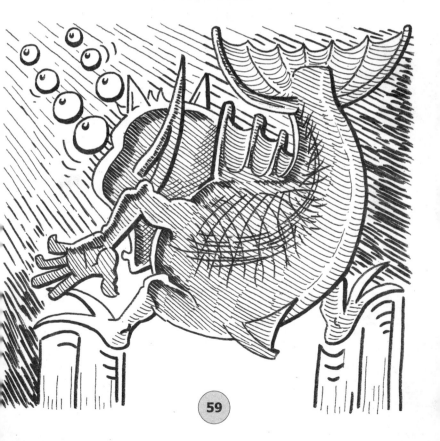

'Maybe it's not true,' said Splat. 'Maybe stars **don't blow up** if we touch them. Maybe the story was just made up!'

'Yipee!' said Fishbum. 'Our very own star. This is wonderful, this is great, this is ... this is ...'

'This is Heaven,' croaked Splat.